For the adorable Maddie Bradley. M.W.
For Robyn Mathison, the Guardian Angel
of Mary Street. R.B.

VIKING

Published by the Penguin Group
Penguin Books Ltd, 27 Wrights Lane, London W8 5TZ, England
Penguin Putnam Inc., 375 Hudson Street, New York, New York 10014, USA
Penguin Books Australia Ltd, Ringwood, Victoria, Australia
Penguin Books Canada Ltd, 10 Alcorn Avenue, Toronto, Ontario, Canada M4V 3B2
Penguin Books (NZ) Ltd, Private Bag 102902, NSMC, Auckland, New Zealand

Penguin Books Ltd, Registered Offices: Harmondsworth, Middlesex, England

On the World Wide Web at: www.penguin.com

First published by Allen & Unwin Pty Ltd 1998
Published in Viking 2000
10 9 8 7 6 5 4 3 2

Text copyright © Margaret Wild, 1998
Illustrations copyright © Ron Brooks, 1998
All rights reserved

The moral right of the author and illustrator has been asserted

Designed by Ron Brooks
Printed and Bound in Hong Kong / China by SCPC

British Library Cataloguing in Publication Data
A CIP catalogue record for this book is available from the British Library

ISBN 0–670–88960–1

This edition produced for
The Book People Ltd, Hall Wood Avenue, Haydock, St Helens WA11 9UL

Rosie and Tortoise

Story by
Margaret Wild

Pictures by
Ron Brooks

TED SMART

Rosie couldn't wait
for her baby brother to be born.

"I'll teach him how to hop,
leap
and run–

just like me!" she told her Mum.

"When is he going to be born, Mum? When?"

"Be patient," said Mum.
"It'll be a while yet."

But she was wrong.
Bobby was born the very next day.
He was the smallest,
weakest little hare ever.

"He only weighs as much as an onion!"
said Mum.

"We'll feed him up," said Dad.

Rosie stared at her tiny brother.
He hardly even seemed to be breathing.
Suddenly she felt as scared as that time
she'd been chased by a fox.

"Would you like to hold him?" said Mum.

"No," said Rosie.

The days went past.

The family took Bobby out in the pram.

to give him some fresh air and sun.

"He's a bit bigger and a bit stronger," said Mum.

"He weighs as much as a potato now!" said Dad.

"Would you like to push the pram, Rosie?"
"No," said Rosie. And she ran after a butterfly.

One morning Mum said,
"Bobby's nearly as heavy as a turnip!"

"It won't be long before he weighs as much as a cauliflower!" said Dad.

But Rosie thought that Bobby looked as sickly as ever. And when Mum asked her to come and rock the cradle, she said "No," and went off to play on the swing.

Later that day Rosie and Dad
went out picking blackberries.
"Rosie," said Dad, "why don't you like Bobby?"
Rosie nearly dropped her basket.
"I do!" she said. "It's just..."
She stopped,
then she whispered,
"He's so tiny,
it makes me scared."

"Come and sit next to me, Rosie," said Dad,
"I want to tell you a story."

"Once upon a time, there was a hare and
a tortoise who were best friends.
One day they went gathering nuts in

the forest, each going their own way,
but at home-time Tortoise couldn't
find Hare anywhere, so he set off alone.

When night fell, he was still plodding on, saying to himself,

'Slow and steady does it, slow and steady
will get me safely home.'

*Little by little, Tortoise made his way
towards the edge of the forest where*

he saw what looked like a yellow moon moving through the trees.

And there, coming to meet him,

was Hare, with a lantern."

Rosie sat quietly, thinking.
When Bobby was born, he'd weighed the same
as an onion. Then a potato, then a turnip.

One of these days he would weigh as much
as a cauliflower, perhaps a cabbage,
even a pumpkin!

Rosie smiled.

"Bobby is slow and steady," she said. "Isn't he?"

"He is," said Dad.

That night
Rosie held her brother
for the first time.

She could feel
his heart beating against hers.

"Hey, Bobby," she said,
"hey there, little Tortoise!"